SURVIVE! is published by Stone Arch Books
A Capstone Imprint
1710 Roe Crest Drive
North Mankato, Minnesota 56003
www.mycapstone.com

Cataloging-in-Publication Data is available at the Library of
Congress website.
ISBN: 978-1-4965-2557-4 (library binding)
ISBN: 978-1-4965-2563-5 (paperback)
ISBN: 978-1-4965-2567-3 (eBook)

Designer: Hilary Wacholz
Design Elements: Shutterstock: Brothers Good, vladis.studio,
frikota, zelimirz, Epsicons, Macrovector

Summary: Kelly roams the outskirts of the forest with her
friends while they attempt to collect various bugs for a science
assignment. Soon, a particularly rare butterfly catches her
eye and she wanders into the woods in hot pursuit until it
suddenly disappears. When Kelly turns back, she realizes she is
completely turned around with no idea how to get back to her
friends. Armed with only a mason jar, a butterfly net, and a
small lunch, Kelly is forced to contend with the dangers of the
wilderness . . .

Printed in China.
007500LEOS16

LOST

A WILD TALE OF SURVIVAL

> BY THOMAS KINGSLEY TROUPE

> ILLUSTRATED BY KIRBI FAGAN

SURVIVE!

STONE ARCH BOOKS
a capstone imprint

TABLE OF CONTENTS

CHAPTER 1

BUGGING OUT

It was nearing the end of summer, and Kelly Gavin had bugs on the brain. In less than a week, she'd be back to school — and she'd barely started her bug project for biology. She'd been warned throughout the summer with e-mail reminders from Mr. Schink. They needed to bring in at least twenty-five different bugs to display and study on the first day of school. She'd deleted each message one by one, thinking she had plenty of time.

"No problem," she said in June. She had collected two specimens and figured she'd get the rest without breaking a sweat.

By the end of July, she had nine specimens. "There's still plenty of time," Kelly told herself.

But now, a week out from school being back in session, she was scrambling to find bugs. They were hard to come by in the city, so all she'd found were a few varieties of ants, a fly, two different mosquitoes, and one of those bugs that looked like a lady bug, but wasn't. Nine in total, which wasn't even half the required amount.

Kelly sat down in a heap next to her best friend, Sasha. "I'm in huge trouble," she said. "I've only got a handful of these dumb bug photos."

Sasha didn't seem worried. Then again, she had caught all of her bugs, photographed, and released them already. She'd been done since June.

Sasha smiled. "Don't fret, Kel," she said. "Come up to the cabin with us this weekend. You'll have all of your bugs in an hour. Maybe faster."

"Awesome!" Kelly said. Her shoulders rotated back and she took in a deep breath.

There were tons of woods around Sasha's cabin at Whisper Lake. "You're a lifesaver!" Kelly said.

Sasha shrugged. "No big deal," she said. "Besides, we'll have a blast once you're done. It's the end of summer, after all!"

* * *

Later that weekend, Kelly stood in the middle of a field armed with the tools Sasha had used months earlier: A small insect net with a fancy wooden handle, a large pickling jar with a metal screw-on lid, and a small pair of padded forceps. And because Kelly wasn't as optimistic as Sasha about being done in an hour, a peanut butter and grape jelly sandwich.

Sasha laid a towel down in the grass and got comfortable. "So you're all set?" she asked, plugging her earbuds into her MP3 player.

Kelly looked around. She wasn't even sure how to start. Kelly had kind of hoped Sasha would help her, but that didn't seem to be part of the plan.

Kelly shrugged. "Um, where should I look?"

"You'll find tons of creepy-crawlies over in those trees," Sasha said, putting her earbuds in. "Just sweep that net around. You'll kick up all kinds of cool bugs."

Kelly got the hint. She'd have to do her own homework. She dropped her cell phone onto the blanket and headed out on her own into the forest.

★ ★ ★

An hour and a half later, Kelly had found twelve more bugs. That left only four remaining bugs to catch. The ones she'd caught were all inside the jar, a buzzing mass of moving legs and antennae. The ones with wings flew around, bouncing against the metal lid. The others squirmed around in a pile at the bottom of their temporary prison.

As she continued along the dirt path beneath the trees, Kelly continued to listlessly sweep her net back and forth along the tall grass. Then she saw a butterfly unlike any she'd ever seen before. It was mostly black with a splash of blue on each of the wings and white speckles at the edges.

That's a winner, Kelly thought, turning to follow it. *If I catch it, Mr. Schink is sure to give me an A.*

Stepping off the dirt path and into the long grass, Kelly followed the butterfly deeper into the woods.

THE CLEARING

When Kelly emerged from the tree line, she found herself in a clearing she hadn't seen in the hundred-some times she'd stayed at Sasha's cabin. It was a whole new field with a rocky hill and large pine trees reaching toward the sky. The ground was littered with broken chunks of trees. Kelly couldn't spot a single sign of a trail or path.

Slowly, the realization set in that Kelly had no idea where she was.

"Don't freak out," Kelly whispered to herself.

Kelly looked around for some sort of landmark from the hundreds of nature walks she, Sasha, and Sasha's little sister, Margo, had taken. Nothing looked familiar.

Kelly fought back the urge to panic, but she had to admit to herself that she was completely lost.

The butterfly, meanwhile, was unaffected by their new location. It fluttered across the field without a care in the world. Kelly silently wished she had wings of her own.

"I'll snag you, then I'll find my way out of here," she said to the butterfly. "The clearing can't be far from here, anyway."

Kelly raised the net and swished it, narrowly missing the butterfly. It bobbed up and down aimlessly. Kelly was pretty sure the dumb bug was toying with her.

"Seriously," Kelly hissed. "Stay still!"

She swung again, missed again, and tripped over an old, rotten piece of wood.

Her chin hit the ground hard. She dropped her bottle. If it shattered, she'd lose all her bugs — and her biology grade would go from A to F. Thankfully, the bottle rolled a few inches and came to a stop against some tufts of grass.

"Phew," Kelly said and stood up.

She brushed the dirt from her knees, rubbed her chin (no blood), and straightened out her khaki shorts. She felt her sandwich squishing in her pocket, but thankfully it was still inside the sealed plastic bag. She looked around only to realize she wasn't even sure what part of the woods she'd emerged from.

Just then, the butterfly flittered into her field of vision. "Forget this," Kelly said to the careless creature. "I'll find a few more bugs when I get back. Some more ants, a different beetle, or something like that."

She headed back toward the line of trees at the edge of the clearing and looked around. Her shoulders sank.

Kelly had been so focused on the butterfly that none of the trees, flora, or anything else looked remotely familiar.

After a few cautious steps into the forest, Kelly stopped.

I didn't wander that far from Sasha, she thought. Her hands started fluttering restlessly at her sides. *Did I?*

CHAPTER 3

LOST?

Kelly scurried through the woods. Her bare legs were covered in scratches, she'd ripped her black shirt on some thorny bushes, and she was slicked with sweat. Mosquitoes buzzed about her head whenever she stopped moving, so she didn't, which only made her sweat more. Which attracted more bugs. A vicious cycle of bug bites and sweat. Sadly, she had no need to collect more mosquitoes.

Kelly still had no idea if she was any closer to where her best friend was. Every part of the woods looked the same to her.

No matter which way she went, it felt like she was just getting farther and farther away from the cabin. *Forget the dumb bugs, Mr. Schick, my grade, and everything else,* she thought. *I just want to be back inside the Jorgensens' cabin.*

"Sasha!" Kelly yelled as loud as she could.

Kelly froze in place, listening carefully in case Sasha called back. A moment passed. Then another. Only weird insect noises called back to her. Deeper in the woods, a bird warbled.

Maybe I should mark a tree or something, Kelly thought. At least then I'll be able to tell if I'm just going in circles. She took the end of the insect net's handle and scraped an *X* into the soft bark of a giant tree.

She took a few steps away, then turned back to see if she could still see the X. *Big enough,* she thought. She scratched another *X* into another nearby tree. "Sorry," she said to it.

Let's just hope I don't see these marks again, Kelly thought.

Kelly continued to mark the bigger trees along the way. As she walked, she listened for the sounds of people at their cabins, boats, or anything that might indicate civilization.

But besides the faint wind whispering through the leaves, it was silent. *Eerily* silent.

"Sasha!" Kelly cried, trying really hard to make it sound like she wasn't panicking. But she *was* panicking — totally and completely. Especially after, once again, no one called back to her.

Kelly smacked herself on the forehead. *You spaz,* she realized. *Of course Sasha can't hear you. She's listening to music!*

Kelly held her bottle of bugs in one hand and the insect net in the other. "So either way, I'm on my own," she whispered, leaning against a tree.

She looked up at the sky and thought about using the sun's movement to find her way back. It was just before noon when she'd entered the forest. When the sun started to set, it would be in the west.

The sun seemed a little off-center to Kelly, which meant that direction was west. And if that was west, then the Jorgensens' cabin was probably south of her current location.

She wasn't completely certain, and heading that way might lead to nowhere — but standing around and doing nothing *would* get her nowhere.

Kelly turned and headed off through the overgrown woods. "South it is, then," she said.

She'd taken ten steps toward "south" when she heard something rustling in the bushes. Before she could even glance over her shoulder, Kelly heard a low growl.

She wasn't alone.

Kelly slowly looked back. A large black bear was about thirty yards behind her. It eyed her carefully and took a few cautious steps forward.

Kelly gasped and froze in place. Slowly, cautiously, she started walking in the opposite direction . . . but the bear kept following her.

The large creature moved extra slowly — like some madman in a horror movie.

The bear grunted. Kelly nearly screamed.

It's calling its bear friends! Kelly thought. She moved more quickly through the underbrush. *It's probably telling the others that it found a delicious city kid.*

Kelly ducked behind a cluster of trees and crouched low. She wrapped her arms around her knees to make herself as small as possible.

Slowly, she peered through the crook of the tree trunk. The bear was coming closer.

"It's coming for me," Kelly said beneath her breath.

Convinced the bear would catch her and maul her if she didn't do something, she ran in the direction she was not entirely sure was south.

CHAPTER 4

ON THE RUN

Kelly swung her insect net to slap low-growing plants out of her path as she ran. She wasn't sure how fast the bear could run or how hungry it was, but she wasn't going to stick around to find out.

She considered ditching the jar of bugs but eventually decided they were worth keeping. At least if she made it out alive, getting lost in the woods wouldn't have been for nothing. Even if she didn't catch that strange butterfly.

Kelly cradled the jar in her armpit and tried not to knock the bugs around too much as she ran.

Kelly thought about shouting for Sasha again but knew it wouldn't do any good — she was probably still listening to music. Besides, Kelly didn't want to let any other bears know she was nearby. With her luck, every hungry bear in the United States would come chasing after her.

Kelly burst through the tree-line, hoping she'd gotten lucky and found the clearing where Sasha was waiting. Instead, she'd returned to the pine tree hill. One of the Xs she'd carved was behind her.

"Great," Kelly muttered. "I've come full circle."

She sprinted through the clearing. A cluster of scared birds took flight, cawing. Kelly watched the birds soar away. It gave her an idea. She picked up speed and headed for the hills. If she could climb a tree, maybe the bear would lose interest in her. And if she climbed high enough, maybe she'd be able to see Whisper Lake! *It's worth a shot,* she thought.

Kelly reached the slope. Larger rocks jutted from the dirt, giving her plenty of handholds. She clenched the handle of the bug net in her teeth.

Kelly used her one free hand to search for roots and rocks. With a quick glance behind her, she saw the bear emerge from the trees about fifty feet away.

Kelly moved quickly but steadily up the hill. After another few feet of climbing, Kelly pulled herself onto a flatter portion of the hill. She noticed a spot behind a few larger rocks where she could easily duck out of sight. Kelly crouched and scanned the clearing. No sign of the bear.

Kelly sat in silence, listening. All she could hear was the beat of her heart in her chest. Then she heard something rustle the leaves near her face. With the end of the pole of her net, she knocked a leaf away from the ground. A centipede zigzagged across the side of the rock.

Kelly took out her forceps and gently snapped up the bug. The insect squirmed and wiggled as she quietly unscrewed her glass jar. "Welcome to the party," Kelly whispered, dropping the centipede in with the rest of the bugs.

She was glad to have a friend — even one as gross as "Legs."

CHAPTER 5

BOTTLED UP

Kelly quietly sat with her back pressed against the rock. She watched the centipede zip around through the other bugs in the jar, wondering if it was as panicked as she was, hoping for a chance to escape and survive.

She knew there was no chance the centipede could get out. The lid was screwed back on, nice and tight. Kelly hoped she had better odds. Slowly, she peeked around the rock again and listened for any other sounds of the bear coming for her. Other than the usual woodsy noises, it was quiet.

Kelly let out a sigh of relief. She looked into her jar again. Legs, the centipede, was slowing down. Kelly couldn't help but feel bad for the crawly thing. "I'm not happy with the way things are turning out for me, either, friend."

She stood up, gripping the insect net like a weapon. There was something mushy pressing against her leg. When she looked down, she saw a purple stain. Her sandwich had squirted grape jelly into her shorts pocket.

"Oh, that's just fantastic," Kelly muttered, then realized she should be quiet. She considered throwing the mashed-up thing away, but decided not to. She had no idea how long she would be lost in the woods. She didn't want to regret throwing away the only food she had.

"Don't worry, Legs," she whispered. "No matter how bad things get, I won't be eating you."

Kelly brushed some of the jelly off her leg and headed up the hill. Farther up, the trees thinned out a little.

Maybe I can spot the lake from there, she thought. She grabbed hold of tree branches and rocks to make her way up the slope.

As she reached the peak, she looked over the horizon. She'd expected to see a big empty spot in the line of trees where the lake was, or maybe even the other cabins near the Jorgensen place. Any place where there were people. People who could help her get out of the woods and back into civilization.

But that's not what Kelly saw. To make matters worse, the bear was slowly clambering up the side of the hill. "No way," she whispered. "Am I being outsmarted by a bear?"

As if in response, the beast made a clicking sound at her and sped up.

"Let's get moving, Legs," Kelly whispered to her collection.

She scrambled up the hill, desperate to put more distance between herself and the bear. She continued climbing, worried she was moving farther away from the cabin, Sasha, and civilization.

CHAPTER 6

CLIMBING

After what seemed like forever, the ground started to level out. Kelly was glad — her legs and arms were sore, and she was soaked with sweat. Her bugs looked pretty out of it, too. One of the poor beetle's legs had broken off.

I'll make it up to you later, little fella, Kelly thought. *If I survive, that is.*

With no time to look back to see if the bear was still in hot pursuit, Kelly dashed through the woods. She kicked through the tall grass, hopped over fallen trees, and ducked beneath low branches — whatever was necessary to keep moving.

To clear a clump of brush, she swung her net and inadvertently caught three different bugs she'd never seen before.

"This net is a lifesaver," she muttered. She slowed down just enough to deposit her new specimens into the jar. With a quick spin of the lid, she locked them inside.

As Kelly tried to figure out which way was south again, she heard a bubbling sound. It was close by. Immediately, she felt a sense of hope surge into her chest. That has to be a stream, she realized. Probably the one that runs underneath the small bridge on the dirt road to the Jorgensens' cabin!

They'd driven over it plenty of times, but she didn't think much of it before now. If she followed it, it'd take her to the road. Then it would be just a half-mile or so to the cabin.

Kelly pumped her fist in the air in silent celebration. *I'm not out of the woods yet,* she thought. Kelly wondered if someone who'd been lost like her had come up with that saying.

Regardless, Kelly knew the stream was her best chance of finding her way back. She ran toward the stream. It snaked its way through the trees and flowed off in a direction she was pretty sure was southeast.

Close enough! she thought.

The bear made a huffing sound from behind her. Kelly looked over her shoulder. The look on the bear's face made her think it was frustrated. *Deal with it,* she thought. *I won't be your snack.*

Kelly recalled a movie where she'd seen where escaping prisoners had hidden in water to mask their scents. The police dogs chasing them couldn't smell them when they were in the water.

It was following me even when it couldn't see me, Kelly thought. *Maybe that's why it's still on my tail.*

Kelly dashed to the edge of the stream. Small rocks poked up through the surface, providing a natural walkway across. Without hesitation, she leapt from one stone to another, doing her best to keep her balance.

Halfway through the stream, Kelly turned to look. The bear reached the edge of the water and paused. Then it bounded into the water and continued after her.

Kelly turned to run but the slick soles of her shoes made her slip. She managed to catch herself before she fell, but now one of her shoes was waterlogged. Great, she thought. Now I'll run even slower.

Kelly was desperate. Perched precariously on top of two rocks, she shifted one foot to get them closer together. As she did, she felt a squish in her pocket.

Her eyes went wide. *That's it!* she realized. *That's why he's following me . . . the sandwich!*

Without another thought, Kelly reached into her shorts pocket, pulled out the sticky sandwich in its bag, and threw it as hard as she could at the bear.

The bag landed with a splat on the bear's head, exploding in a mess of hot peanut butter and jelly.

CHAPTER 7

THE CURRENT

Kelly remembered what had happened the first time she'd visited the Jorgensens' cabin. She'd left a plate of half-finished chicken wings on a picnic table, and Sasha's mom had yelled at her for leaving it out. "You want bears?" she'd said, half joking but still serious. "Because that's how you get bears!"

As Kelly watched the bear splash its way out of the stream and turn its attention to the sandwich on its face, it all began to make sense. *The dumb bear just wanted my food,* Kelly thought. *It didn't want to eat me at all! Well, probably not.*

At that moment, Kelly's balancing act ended —
and she fell with a splash into the stream.

Kelly kicked and swam until she broke the surface
of the cold water. The stream was a lot deeper than
she'd thought. She treaded water until she regained
her orientation. She looked up and saw the bear was
farther away from her already. Everything was. The
current was pulling her away.

Kelly realized she lost her jar in the fall, but she
didn't have the time or energy to think about her
lost jar of bugs. Sure, her collection was one bug
short of being complete. But if she died, it wouldn't
matter what grade she got. The stream's surprisingly
strong current was pulling her downstream — fast.

At least it's taking me away from the bear, Kelly
thought. The next moment, the current pulled her
underwater. She thrashed her legs and felt a few
more rocks scratch her. With a quick foot plant,
Kelly pushed herself up and broke the water's
surface once again.

The bear was the least of her worries now.

There was nothing to hold on to and the current was growing stronger. If she couldn't keep her head above water, she'd drown.

Kelly flipped over onto her back and pointed her feet downstream. She managed to keep her head up somehow while floating on her back. Her head constantly ducked beneath the water, then emerged again. She inhaled mouthfuls of water despite her best efforts to save her breaths for when her head was above the surface.

Farther ahead, she heard the sound of water crashing. Struggling to lean forward, Kelly saw that the stream dropped off ahead.

In a matter of seconds, she'd be going over the edge of a waterfall. And from the sounds and speed of the water, it was a large one.

Kelly flipped onto her stomach and struggled to swim to either side of the shore, but she couldn't fight the current. Still clutching the insect net, she swung it out, hoping to snag one of the rocks on the bank.

As luck would have it, the metal ring caught one on her second swing. She stopped moving downstream! She placed one hand over the other, slowly pulling herself closer . . . until the rock came loose.

Kelly knew she had precious seconds to act. As her leg struck another rock, she dove below the surface. She held the net underwater, gripping each end of the stick as tightly as she could. She felt the stick strike several rocks on the stream's floor. Kelly kicked her feet and swung the net around, hoping to slow herself down and snag one of the rocks.

The rumble of the water grew louder with each passing second. Her lungs burned. The water around her moved even more quickly. She was being swept closer and closer to the waterfall's edge.

Then Kelly felt her legs slip over the edge.

CHAPTER 8

THE EDGE

Kelly felt a strong tug at her arms, and her body stopped moving. She raised her head and broke the surface of the stream, gasping for air. The sound around her was almost deafening. She had managed to hook her net on a giant rock at the end of the stream. The rod kept her in place, dangling at the top of the waterfall.

Gathering what remained of her courage, she looked below. It was at least a thirty-foot drop, and the stream below was riddled with even more stones. There was no way she'd survive the drop.

Kelly clenched her fingers around the rod even tighter. She turned her head to avoid being pelted in the eyes and mouth with water, trying to find a way up and out of the stream before her arms gave out or the stick broke.

Using her feet, Kelly found footholds in the rocky wall beneath her. With a mighty push, she was able to shove her way back up the edge.

As the water slammed into her face, her hand found another rock embedded into the ground. She grabbed it and then pulled herself a little closer to the shore.

Despite every instinct screaming for her to hurry, hurry, hurry, Kelly moved slowly and carefully, testing each rock for stability before placing any weight on it.

Slowly, inch by inch, she edged her way onto the stream's bank.

When she was able to finally stand up, Kelly nearly collapsed from exhaustion. And hunger.

"Stupid bear . . . even got . . . my sandwich," Kelly said between gasps. She glanced back to where the bear was. He was wiping PB&J off his face with his long tongue. The bear gave her one final glance, then sauntered away.

Kelly let out a sigh of relief. She shook the insect net dry, reminding herself to thank Sasha's parents for not buying a cheap one.

She spent the next hour slowly making her way down the hill. She was careful not to let the stream leave her sight. When Kelly was on lower ground, she walked along the shore and netted a few bugs. She even caught herself a dragonfly.

After what seemed like hours, she finally found the bridge that the Jorgensens' truck had driven over to get to their cabin. Just below the bridge, something glinted in the sunlight.

Kelly almost exploded into a fit of laughter. Banging against one of the wooden posts and bobbing in the water was her insect jar. By some miracle the jar had not shattered.

Kelly picked it up and unscrewed the cap. She dumped in the five extra bugs she'd found on her way back, adding them to the collection.

"Thanks for waiting, Legs," Kelly said. "Here's the rest of the party."

Sealing up her collection, Kelly rested the insect net on her shoulder. She climbed out of the ditch and onto the gravel road. Despite the day's events, she was grinning from ear to ear.

★ ★ ★

When Kelly finally reached the Jorgensens' cabin, Sasha's little sister Margo saw her first.

"Holy cow, Kelly!" Margo cried. "What happened to you?"

Kelly limped her way toward the cabin's deck. "Oh, nothing serious," she said flatly. "Got lost in the woods, chased by a bear, and nearly went over the edge of a waterfall. Found all my bugs, though."

Kelly picked up her cell phone she'd left behind. She took a few photos of all the bugs in the jar.

With proof of her finished homework safely in her photo gallery on her phone, Kelly let out a sigh of relief.

Kelly lifted the jar off the table, opened the lid, and lay it on its side in the grass. "There," she said, smiling. "You're free, fellas."

Legs was the last one to crawl to freedom. For a moment, it seemed to Kelly that the little bug was waving goodbye. "Later, Legs," she said.

"Ew!" Margo squealed, lifting her dangling feet up from her chair.

Kelly laughed. "Don't worry," she said, making a funny face at Margo. "I'll protect you from the creepy-crawlies."

Margo giggled — but kept her feet tucked underneath her. "So . . . did the bear attack you?" she asked.

"Nope," Kelly said, collapsing in a deck chair next to Margo. "The hungry jerk just followed me for a few miles."

"Oh. That must be Reggie," Margo said. "Reggie's super friendly. He loves people food. Most bears won't bother people, you know." Margo delivered the last line like a squeaky version of her mother, Mrs. Jorgensen.

Kelly smirked and playfully rustled Margo's curls. "Now you tell me," she said.

WILDERNESS SURVIVAL

The best way to survive the wilderness is to not get lost! Proper preparation for your woodland adventures is absolutely vital for survival — and avoiding areas with bears is necessary; at best, bears are unpredictable and dangerous.

Clothing: Staying warm and dry is vital. Thick-soled boots, waterproof clothing, and clothes that cover your skin will go a long way to shield you from poisonous plants and bug bites. (Don't forget the bug spray.)

Fluids: Staying hydrated is crucial, especially during long trips in warm weather. It is not safe to depend on streams or lakes for drinking water, so make sure to bring plenty of water in bottles or canteens.

Compass or GPS: A compass will point you in the right direction as long as you know where you need to go. A GPS is better — as long as you're sure it'll work where you'll be traveling.

Flashlight: If night falls, you'll be in bad shape without a flashlight (and no, the one on your cell phone isn't going to cut it). Make sure you have the correct type of batteries — and some spares.

Shelter: In case of inclement weather, be sure you know where to find shelter. And if you plan on camping, make sure you know how to set up your tent!

Cell Phone: Make sure you check your cell phone carrier's coverage areas beforehand if you plan to depend on it in the wilderness. While some people think cell phones "ruin" the wilderness experience, it's better to have one (even if it's turned off) in case you need it. With that said, rescue teams often take quite a bit of time to arrive after a call, so be sure to follow the previously mentioned precautions in case you end up having to wait for a while.

ABOUT THE AUTHOR

Thomas Kingsley Troupe has written more than thirty children's books. His book *Legend of the Werewolf* (Picture Window Books, 2011) received a bronze medal for the Moonbeam Children's Book Award. Thomas lives in Woodbury, Minnesota, with his wife and two boys.

ABOUT THE ILLUSTRATOR

Kirbi Fagan is a vintage-inspired artist living in the Detroit, Michigan, area. She is an award-winning illustrator who specializes in creating art for young readers. Her work is known for magical themes, vintage textures, bright colors, and powerful characterization. She received her bachelor's degree in Illustration from Kendall College of Art and Design. Kirbi lives by two words: "Spread joy." She is known to say, "I'm in it with my whole heart." When not illustrating, Kirbi enjoys writing stories, spending time with her family, and rollerblading with her dog, Sophie.

GLOSSARY

antennae (an-TEN-uh)—thin, sensitive organs on the head of an insect

crook (KROOK)—a curved or hooked part of something

emerged (i-MERJD)—rose up or out from something, or appeared

flora (FLOHR-uh)—plants

jutted (JUT-id)—stuck up, out, or forward

inadvertently (in-ad-VER-tuhnt-lee)—not intended or planned

landmark (LAND-mark)—an object or structure on land that is easy to see and recognize

maul (MAWL)—attack or injure in a violent way

specimen (SPESS-uh-muhn)—something that is collected for studying, like an animal or plant

WRITING PROMPTS

1. Based on what you've learned from the survival tips after the end of this story, create a list of things Kelly could have done differently to stay safer on her wilderness adventure.

2. Rewrite a page of this story from the bear's perspective. Knowing what you learned about Reggie the bear at the end of the story, explain what he's thinking as he follows Kelly through the woods.

3. Write a short story about surviving a difficult situation of some kind. How will you make it out alive? Describe your adventure.